May the blessings of the
Lord be with you always.

JACY'S Search For Jesus

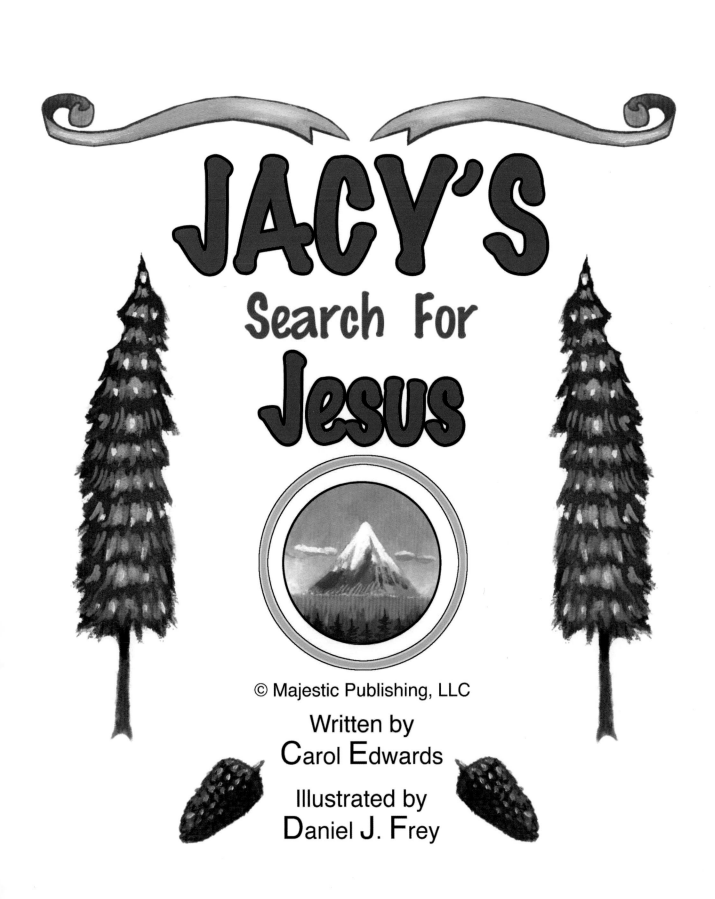

Written by
Carol Edwards

Illustrated by
Daniel J. Frey

Majestic Publishing, LLC,
PO Box 1560, Atlanta, GA 30058.

ISBN-13: 978-0-9755314-0-2
ISBN-10: 0-9755314-0-9

Published by Majestic Publishing, LLC, Atlanta, GA 30058

Printed in the U.S.A.

www.majesticpublishing.net

Book Design by Daniel J. Frey
www.nois.com/frey/frey.htm

In Loving Memory of my mother
Fannie M. Edwards

Jacy was thrilled and scared all at the same time. He loved it when he and his mother went flying. He would hop on her back and she would soar high above the trees and the clouds. Although Jacy had flown with his mother many times, and they always followed the same routine, she could still surprise him. Suddenly, his mother would drop him and he would go crashing towards the ground at record speed. Frightened as Jacy was, he still had fun. He would flap his little wings, but it wouldn't help him. He knew he would be okay anyway, because his mother never let him fall. She would swoop down, stretch out her wings, and grab him. It was all part of learning to fly, and Jacy couldn't wait until he could soar high into the sky on his own.

"Mom, why can't I fly? Other birds my age are starting to fly."

"Well, Jacy, other eagles your age are a little bigger than you are. Their wings have developed a bit more than yours," said his mother.

"What's taking my wings so long? And when will I get bigger like the other eagles?" Jacy asked anxiously.

"Jacy, just be patient. Everyone and everything develops in its own time."

"You always say that. I'm ready now!" Jacy shouted.

"I know, sweetie. You will fly when it's time—I promise you," said his mother in a very soft voice.

"You promise?"

His mother held up one wing and said "I promise."

His mother always made him feel better. And he loved it when she read him stories. She did that a lot when he felt a little sad. His mother read him many kinds of stories, but he liked the bible stories about Jesus best.

One night, after Jacy's mother read him a story, a heavy rain began to fall. Even though eagles usually build nests in very high places, their nest was in one of the shortest trees in the forest. Jacy's mother thought they would be safer in a short tree because of the many windy storms in their forest. And it worked most of the time, but on this night, the storm was fierce. Jacy would never forget the piercing sound of the thunder. The bright lightning illuminated the whole forest. The strong wind knocked down trees all over the forest.

Then their tree and nest started to fall! Jacy's mother stretched out her wings to catch him, as she had done so many times before, but just as she touched him, another strong gust of wind came. It blew Jacy all the way to the other side of the forest. Jacy had no idea where he was. He had never been separated from his mother before. What was he to do? He began to cry. Then he thought he heard something, like a small voice. Only a little louder than a whisper, it sounded a lot like his mother's voice saying, "Remember what I taught you, Jacy. If we ever become separated, look for Jesus. Jesus will never leave you. He will take care of you."
Jacy looked around, but he didn't see anyone.
Was that truly his mother's voice he heard?
Jacy wasn't sure, but he stopped crying. He felt a little better.

Jacy looked up to the sky, and then started back to the other side of the forest. But the forest is a huge place. He wasn't sure which direction would get him home. The noises he heard in the forest frightened him. Jacy was not used to being all alone, so he started to cry again. As soon as he laid his head on the ground, he heard his mother's voice again, saying, "It's okay to cry. Jesus bottles up all our tears." Jacy cried himself to sleep.

Jacy woke the next morning feeling refreshed and ready to start the day. He walked for what seemed like miles. Everything in the forest looked the same. He felt as though he wasn't getting anywhere.

His little legs were not used to walking so much, and now he was getting hungry. Jacy didn't know the first thing about hunting for food. His mother always took care of that. But now that he was on his own, he knew he had better learn fast. *If I could only fly*, he thought. He could cover more ground and surely he would be closer to Jesus up there. But Jacy couldn't fly. He continued on his journey until he saw a squirrel about to climb a tree. He said, "Excuse me, Mr. Squirrel. I seem to have lost my way. I'm looking for Jesus. Have you seen Him?"

The squirrel said, "Why are you looking for Jesus?"

"I'm lost, and my mother said if I couldn't find my way back home, I should always look for Jesus. She said that He would look after me, and I wouldn't have to be afraid anymore, but she never told me exactly where Jesus lives."

"Well, what does this Jesus look like?" said the squirrel.

"I'm not really sure," Jacy said.

"Well, how are you supposed to find him?" remarked the squirrel.

"I'm not sure of that, either," replied Jacy.

"The name 'Jesus' does sound a little familiar, but I don't think I know him. You may want to ask Ossie Owl. He knows almost everyone in the forest. He may know where you can find this Jesus."

"Where can I find Ossie Owl?" asked Jacy.

"Well, Ossie usually doesn't come out until nightfall. You will have to go deeper into the forest. Look for a huge black tree that slopes to the side, and at the very top of the slope you will see Ossie Owl."

Jacy thanked Mr. Squirrel and went deeper into the forest to find Ossie. By the time he got there, the sun was setting. He found the huge black tree with no problem. He looked up at the very top of the slope, but he didn't see Ossie Owl. When he looked down, to his surprise, he saw a puddle filled with worms. You don't have to do much hunting to catch worms, so that was an easy meal for Jacy. *I'll just wait right here*, he thought, but it was getting later and later. Jacy simply could not keep his eyes open any longer and he fell asleep. He woke when he heard a noise: "Oooh…Oooh…." He looked up, and at the very top of the slope was Ossie.

Jacy said, "You must be Ossie Owl. I'm hoping you will be able to help me. I've lost my way and I'm looking for Jesus. I was told you know everyone in the forest. Do you know where I can find Jesus?"

"Tell me what you know about this Jesus. What does He look like?" asked Ossie.

"I don't know what He looks like because I've never seen Him. All I know is He lives somewhere in the sky. If I could only fly, I could probably find Him. You can fly, Ossie. Have you seen him up there anywhere?"

"I don't recall meeting anyone named Jesus," replied Ossie.

"You've just got to know where I can find Him!" cried Jacy.

"Why are you in such an all-fired hurry to find this Jesus, anyway?" Ossie asked.

"I've gotten separated from my mother and I can't find my way home.

My mother always told me that if ever she weren't around, Jesus would be there. She said Jesus is everywhere, but I can't seem to find Him anywhere. Someone around here must know Him, or at least something about Him."

"Let me think a minute," replied Ossie.

"Nope. Sorry, can't help you."

Jacy was disappointed, but he thanked Ossie and went on his way.

As soon as daybreak came the next day, Jacy started walking once again. He just couldn't understand why no one seemed to know where to find Jesus. His mother talked about Jesus with such love that he just couldn't imagine anyone not knowing Him. Especially if they heard about all the wonderful things Jesus did for us. He remembered his mother reading the story of "Daniel in the Lion's Den." It told how Jesus watched over Daniel and wouldn't let the lion eat him. Although Jacy felt alone in the forest, he also felt that Jesus was not far away.

If I can just keep going I'm bound to run into Him sooner or later, he thought.

Jacy grew tired. He had no idea where he was. Then, when he stopped to rest, Paulie Pony happened by.

Paulie said, "It looks like you could use a lift. Where're you headed?"

Jacy looked at Paulie and said, "I've never seen a pony in the forest before."

"I've never been in the forest before," replied Paulie.

"It's the strangest thing. I went out for my afternoon trot and the next thing I knew, I was here. It beats me how I got all the way out here."

"I was getting pretty tired," Jacy said.

"Where're you headed?" Paulie repeated his earlier question.

"I've lost my way and I'm trying to find Jesus," replied Jacy.

"Do you know where I can find Him?"

Paulie stared at Jacy for a while, then said, "Hop on, little guy. I'll give you a lift. Jesus, eh? Yes, I've heard that name before. I'll tell you. One night I trotted past a campsite where there was a lot of talking going on, and I stopped to listen. There was a group sitting in a circle, and they were all reading from a book. I don't know the name of the book—I think it started with a B—but like I said, I stopped to listen. I didn't quite understand all of it. Truth be told, I hardly understood any of it, but it was interesting, so I stayed to the end. At first they talked about this Jesus fellow, but I didn't hear much about Him because they were finishing up talking about Him. Then they started talking about this Noah fellow and something about an Ark. They talked about how Noah built the Ark and all this rain was coming. Do you know what else they were saying about Noah? He got all kinds of animals together, two of every kind, and lots of food, too, and put it all in that Ark. You know, they say it rained for forty days and forty nights—imagine that!

Sure was an interesting story. I don't know how that ties into that Jesus fellow, though."

Jacy said, "I bet Jesus had something to do with all that rain."

"I bet you're right, little guy. I just bet he did."

"Like I said, I was just passing through, but I think there's something about this Jesus. I believe your mother was right about Him. Don't stop looking for Him, because I have a feeling that, when you find Him, your life will never be the same." Jacy told Paulie that the book they had been reading was the Bible. He knew this because his mother had read to him from it.

Paulie stopped and said, "This is as far as I go, little guy. I need to get back to my neck of the woods. Sure beats me how I got all the way out here."

"You know, I bet Jes….never mind. Thanks for the lift," Jacy said.

"I hope to see you again sometime," Paulie said. And they went their separate ways.

Jacy was on his own again, but this time he didn't feel so alone. He sat for hours, and then, out the blue, a song came to him.

Jesus loves me, this I know,
For the Bible tells me so.
Yes, Jesus loves me.
Yes, Jesus loves me.
Yes, Jesus loves me.
For the Bible tells me so.

His mother used to sing him that song. He missed her very much. He felt his mother's presence, and it was so strong that somehow he knew that he would see his mother again. He also knew Jesus would have something to do with it. He looked up to the sky, and journeyed on.